D0821494

MAVIS MAKES A FRIEND

Adapted by **Sheila Sweeny Higginson**

Ready-to-Read

Simon Spotlight

New York   London   Toronto   Sydney   New Delhi

SIMON SPOTLIGHT
An imprint of Simon & Schuster Children's Publishing Division
1230 Avenue of the Americas, New York, New York 10020
This Simon Spotlight edition December 2018
TM & © 2018 Sony Pictures Animation, Inc. All Rights Reserved.
For information about special discounts for bulk purchases, please contact
Simon & Schuster Special Sales at 1-866-506-1949 or
business@simonandschuster.com.
Manufactured in the United States of America 1118 LAK
10 9 8 7 6 5 4 3 2 1
ISBN 978-1-5344-3259-8 (hc)
ISBN 978-1-5344-3258-1 (pbk)
ISBN 978-1-5344-3260-4 (eBook)

Mavis knows how to take
care of things.
She learned from the best!
Her dad, Dracula, is the
most caring vampire in
Transylvania.

Mavis wants to prove she can take care of something.
She sees that Quasimodo has an egg—and he's ready to smash it.

"You can't break that egg!" Mavis shouts.
"I will raise it!"

Quasimodo warns Mavis.
"That is a rotten egg.
It will eat you when it hatches."

Mavis takes the egg anyway.
She makes sure her room is safe.
Spiderwebs block the closet doors.
Blobburgers cushion sharp spikes.

Mavis builds a soft nest of blankets.
Then she sits on the egg to keep it
warm.
"I'm taking care of you, Weggsley,"
Mavis says,
"if it's the last thing I do."

Pedro, Hank, and Wendy are going bowling.
They want Mavis to go, too.

Mavis says, "No way!"
She has to take care of Weggsley.

Mavis is not just good at taking care of Weggsley. She is great at it!

Suddenly, Mavis hears a sound.
Crack!

Mavis shouts as the egg hatches.
"Weggsley, you're a real boy!"

Mavis shows Weggsley how to play
ball. What a catch!
Mavis shows Weggsley how to swim.
Look at him float!

Mavis shows Weggsley how to write his name.
She is so proud of her good little egg!

"I have a greater purpose in my undead life now," Mavis says proudly.

Her friends are worried that Mavis
might not have an undead life much
longer.

"Mavis, you heard Quasi," Wendy
warns her friend.

"Weggsley's a bad egg!"

"Look, he needs me," Mavis tells her friends. "When you have an egg with legs one day, you'll understand."

Pedro and Hank only understand one thing. Weggsley might be dangerous. "No, he's not," Mavis tells them. "He is the sweetest, cutest egg you could ever ask for."

At bedtime
Mavis tells Weggsley a story.

". . . All the king's ghouls and undead men couldn't put Humpty together again."

"Sorry!" Mavis says. "I can't believe I just read that to you."

Weggsley covers his face with his feet.

"Aw, Weggsley wants to play creep-a-boo," Mavis says.

Mavis covers her eyes.
Then she moves her hands and makes
a scary face.

"CREEP-A-BOOOOO!" she shouts.

Weggsley is gone!

Mavis races out of her room.
She dashes down the hall to look
for him.
"WEGGGGGSLEY!" she cries.

Mavis races to the kitchen.
Weggsley is chopping vegetables.

"Weggsley!" Mavis says as she scoops her egg up. "Be careful!"

Weggsley doesn't want to be careful, though.
He wiggles right out of Mavis' arms!
Mavis chases him to the piranha tanks . . . and across the shelves.

They jump over a mountain of veggies.
Mavis ends up in the cauldron!

Pedro, Hank, and Wendy try to warn Mavis.

"It is a *bad egg*!" Quasimodo shouts.

"He's just playing make-believe," Mavis replies.

Weggsley stirs the pot with a giant spoon.

He is not playing.

He is ready to make Mavis into soup!

Mavis turns into a bat.
She flies out of the pot.

Weggsley sprouts wings and flies after her!

Weggsley is close enough to catch her.
It looks like the end for Mavis, until . . .
Gulp!
A hungry Venus flytrap swallows
Weggsley whole!
Mavis swoops down near the moat.

Relieved, Mavis flies back to her friends.

"Sorry about your egg," Hanks says.

"I guess Weggsley was a bad egg after all," Mavis admits.

"If only somebody had warned me!"

"If only . . ." Wendy laughs. "If only!"